A *Little, Brown* Book

First published in Great Britain in 1992
by Little, Brown and Company

A CIP catalogue record for this book is available from
the British Library.

ISBN 0 316 90394 9

Printed and bound in Italy by Graphicom SRL.

Little, Brown and Company (UK) Limited
165 Great Dover Street
London SE1 4YA

Clangers

The Music Trees

STORY BY OLIVER POSTGATE
PICTURES BY PETER FIRMIN

LITTLE, BROWN AND COMPANY

It was night-time on the little blue moon where the Clangers live.

Here on Earth, where you and I live, we know when it is night-time because it gets dark, but on the Clangers' moon it never gets dark. So the Clangers, who need their sleep just like we do, have invented their own night-time.

On the wall of their living-cave there is a special clock. When the hand of the clock points upwards to the six dots, Mother Clanger calls out, "Night-time! Sleep-time! Everybody to bed!"

Then all the Clangers curl up into round balls, pull their ears over their eyes and roll into their soft bed-caves. Mother Clanger comes round to tuck them in, to say good-night and close the flaps.

Tiny Clanger lay in her bed-cave. She was wide awake. She had had such an exciting day that she couldn't sleep. The Iron Chicken had visited them and had given her an iron egg as a present. Tiny Clanger was very pleased to be given such an interesting present but she was also wondering quite seriously what she was going to do with it. You see, an iron egg is not really what you would call a *useful* sort of present.

As she lay there listening to the other Clangers snoring, Tiny Clanger realised that she could hear another sound as well.

She sat up and listened. Yes, she could hear small sweet notes of music. They were not quite a tune but they were the sort of sounds that you could put together and make a tune out of.

Where were they coming from?

Tiny Clanger lifted the flap of her bed-cave and looked out. Everything in the living-cave seemed to be the same as usual.

Very quietly Tiny Clanger slipped out of her bed-cave and crept down to where the iron egg was lying beside the dinner-block. She put her ear to it. Yes, she could hear the faint muffled notes of music coming from inside it.

"I wonder if there is a way to open it," she thought.

Tiny rolled the egg over.

Then something terrible happened. The egg went on rolling. The floor was on a slope and, once it had started to roll, the egg rolled faster and faster until it came to the white quarry.

It rolled straight over the edge and fell with a loud clunking clatter on to the floor of the quarry.

Tiny Clanger ran down and looked over. The egg had broken clean in half, and out of it had fallen a handful of things that looked like little black sticks with knobs on the ends.

Tiny picked one of them up. "I wonder if the music was made by these," she said to herself. She tapped it gently on the side of her nose and . . .

Pling . . . the black knob glowed for a moment and rang like a tiny bell.

Tiny Clanger tried another one . . .

Plang . . . a different note!

"Notes of music!" she whistled. "That's what they are!"

Tiny Clanger knew how to set out notes of music. She drew five straight lines on the white wall of the quarry and placed the notes in order, from left to right, with the high notes on the upper lines and the low notes on the lower lines.

Then she stood back and pointed to each note, starting from the left. As she pointed to it, each note glowed for a moment and played . . .

Pling,
       plang,   *pling, a-plang,*
               pling-plong-plang,
                                      PLONG!

"Eeek!" whistled Tiny Clanger. "I have written a tune!"
Quite forgetting that it was the middle of the night, Tiny Clanger ran back to the bed-caves squeaking like a steam-whistle, "Small! Small! Come quickly! I have written a tune!"

Small Clanger lifted the flap of his bed-cave.
"What are you talking about?" he asked sleepily.
"The iron egg!" said Tiny. "I thought it was no use at all but it was full of notes of music. I wrote a tune with them."
"Where is it now?"
"It rolled away and broke in half in the white quarry. Come on, run!"

Small and Tiny ran to the edge of the quarry and looked down.

The two halves of the egg were still there but the notes which Tiny Clanger had put on the wall were all gone – or almost all. The Soup Dragon was just reaching out her long green neck to eat the last two. She had eaten all the others.

Tiny Clanger jumped down and pushed her away.

"You are a bad, bad dragon!" she whistled. "You have eaten my tune!"

"Very nice, very nice, I am very fond of music," said the Soup Dragon.

Well, as you know, the Soup Dragon usually has an urgly-burbly sort of voice. It is never easy to understand what she says, but now that she had eaten the notes of music her voice was quite different. It had become pure music.

"Plinka-plinka plingaplang poo!" was what she said, and
that was quite impossible to understand.

"Plang, plang, pling!" she added, and stepped neatly
round Tiny Clanger in order to reach the last two notes.

Tiny Clanger was too quick for her. She grabbed the two
notes, threw them on the floor and before the Soup
Dragon could reach them she rolled half of the iron egg on
top of them like a lid.

Then she and Small Clanger sat on it.

"*Pling, plang?*" asked the Soup Dragon.

"Go away!" shouted Small and Tiny.

"*Oh, plong, plong, pling-plang!*" said the Dragon, looking very disappointed. "*Plong, plinkety pooh?*"

"No, you can't," shouted Small and Tiny. "Go away!"

"*Oh ploo!*" muttered the Soup Dragon crossly and she ambled away towards her soup wells.

Small and Tiny lifted off the half-egg and picked up the notes.

Tiny tapped one of them and Small tapped the other . . .
Plong!
Plong!
They were deep, sad notes.

"Those are no use," said Tiny Clanger sadly. "You can't make a tune with just two notes. We might as well throw them away or feed them to the Soup Dragon. What use are two notes of music?"

Then Small Clanger had an idea. He jumped in the air and squeaked, "I know!"

Small Clanger picked up the notes and ran up to the nearest outside-lid. He pushed it with his nose and it clanged open. He climbed out on to the curved outside of the planet.

Tiny Clanger followed him, feeling very puzzled. She watched him walk carefully across the crumbly pale blue ground until he found a sheltered spot.

There he dug a hole with his foot and dropped one of the notes into it.

"You are planting them!" cried Tiny Clanger.

"That's right," said Small Clanger as he dropped the other note into another hole and filled it in. "Now they will grow. You watch!"

They sat on a little hill and watched.

Nothing happened.

A cloud (or rather, *the* cloud, because it was the only cloud there was) floated over and watched with them.

Still nothing happened.

"That's no use," said Tiny Clanger at last. "Music notes are not like seeds. They don't grow if you plant them."

"How do you know?" asked Small. "They may just need watering."

Small Clanger walked over to the cloud and looked at it.

"I'll tell you what," he said to Tiny Clanger. "You climb on my back and see if you can blow the cloud over to the notes. Then it might rain on them."

Tiny Clanger stood on Small Clanger's back and stretched out her long thin nose.

Puff . . . puff . . . puff!

She blew as hard as she could but the cloud did not move at all. As a matter of fact the cloud didn't move because it didn't want to move. It didn't want to be blown about by Clangers. It liked to float about by itself.

Puff . . . puff . . . puff!

Feeling rather cross, the cloud lifted up its end and bumped it down rather heavily on the tip of Tiny Clanger's nose . . .

Puff . . . splonk!

It was a very solid sort of cloud and Clangers' noses are very sensitive.

Tiny squeaked and fell off. Small Clanger picked her up and patted her bumped nose.

"That was a rotten thing to do!" he said to the cloud. "All we wanted was to ask you to rain some raindrops on the music notes we just planted."

It was really a friendly sort of cloud. All it wanted was to be asked, politely. It floated over to the seeds and rained a small shower of raindrops which fell like tiny clear notes of music on to the blue ground.

"Thankyou, Cloud," said Small Clanger. "Now they will grow."

"No they won't," said Tiny Clanger. "They would have to be magic to grow."

Well, perhaps they were magic notes because almost at once they heard a tiny *ping!* and a black dot appeared on the ground.

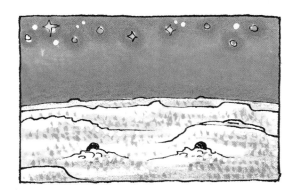 

Ping! . . . Another dot appeared.
Ping, ping, ping-ping-ping . . . Up came two thin stalks.
Plinga, planga, plonga . . . The stalks grew branches.

Pinkety-pinkety, pinkety-pinkety, pinkety-pinkety, ping!
. . . Tiny white flowers grew all along the branches.

Plong, plong, plong, plong-plong, plang . . . The flowers
fell, leaving lines of perfect music notes hanging from the
branches.

Tiny Clanger picked up a straw-stick and bowed to the
music trees. Then she lifted her stick and, just as if she was
conducting an orchestra, she pointed to each note in turn.
And, just like a tiny orchestra, the notes on the music trees
played her a tune.

At the end of the tune she bowed again and several Clangers, who had come quietly out to listen, clapped and whistled for more.

Then the music trees played a tune for Small Clanger and this time the cloud joined in, dropping little raindrops which rang like tiny bells.

When they had finished the Clangers clapped and whistled until Mother Clanger put her head out and reminded them, quite crossly, that it was the middle of the night and time all good Clangers were asleep in their bed-caves.

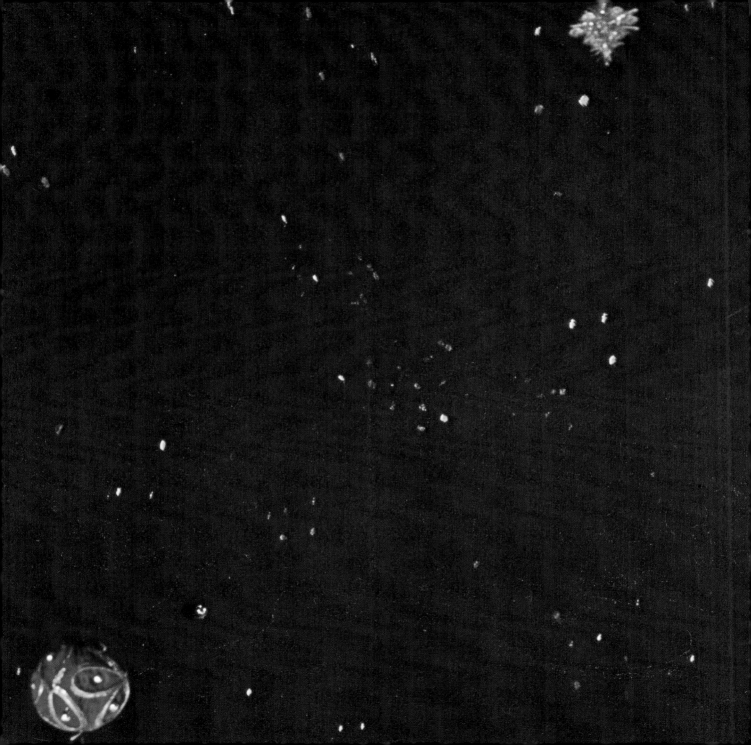